Funny Bone

CHRISTOPHER STITT

Illustrated by Nathan Jurevicius

 sundance

The Story Characters

Rick

Dad

Sarah

Grandpa

James

The Story Setting

Circus

School Library

James's House

Rick's House

Grandpa's House

TABLE OF CONTENTS

CHAPTER 1

I Lost My Funny Bone

My dad took me to the circus. He thought that the clowns were really funny.

He laughed so hard that he started to snort.

"Stop it, Dad," I said.

Dad rolled around laughing and snorting. He slapped my back and sent my popcorn flying. I was really mad.

"What's wrong, Rick? Lost your funny bone?" he laughed.

Can you lose your funny bone? Had I
really lost my funny bone?

Clowns are supposed to be funny.
But I just couldn't laugh.

Where had my funny bone gone? Was it hiding? What did it look like? How could I find it if I didn't know what it looked like?

I worried all the way home.

Dad chuckled to himself for the whole trip. "That clown was so funny!"

CHAPTER 2

Was It Hiding?

I tried to figure out where my funny bone might hide. My big sister, Sarah, was watching TV. Her silly laughs were really annoying me.

"This is the funniest show I've ever seen. Don't you think so, Rick?"

I didn't laugh. I just got up and left.

"What's wrong, Rick? Lost your funny bone?"

Even Sarah knew I'd lost my funny bone.

I went to my room and looked for my funny bone.

I searched under the bed. It wasn't there. I searched in the closet. There wasn't any room in there.

I searched in the toy box. No luck at all. I searched the dirty clothes basket. Nothing would hide in there.

I worried all night.

The next day, I went to the school library. I wanted to find a picture of a funny bone. It would be easier to find if I knew what it looked like.

What Does It Look Like?

The next day, I went to the school library. I wanted to find a picture of a funny bone. It would be easier to find if I knew what it looked like.

It was no use. I couldn't find a picture anywhere.

I guessed that a funny bone would
look really weird.

It had to be funny and do goofy things.

A funny bone would laugh a lot.
Maybe I would hear it.

My friend, James, came over. "What are you doing, Rick?" he asked.

"Looking for something," I said.

"I hope it's your funny bone," said James.

"How did you know?" I said.

"You must have lost it. You were the only one who didn't laugh at the school puppet show today."

I felt so bad. Even my friends had noticed that my funny bone was missing.

I had to set a trap to catch it.

CHAPTER 4

It's Not Funny!

That night, my grandpa came for dinner. He always tells jokes.

I didn't listen. I was too worried.

"What's wrong, Rick? You always laugh at my jokes. Lost your funny bone?"

"Yes! I have!" I yelled. I ran up to my room and slammed the door.

I've got to catch that funny bone, I thought.

I needed my large fishing net to do
this job.

CHAPTER 5

Hunting a Funny Bone

I searched the house from top to bottom.

When I went into the kitchen, I heard a
funny noise. "Hah, hah, hah, snort . . .
hah, hah, hah, snort . . . hah, hah, hah,
snort . . ."

Who was laughing? Maybe it was my
funny bone. It sounded just like a
funny bone.

I lifted my net. I brought it down on
something lumpy. Then I caught my
funny bone.

Well, I thought I did. It was really my dad.

He wasn't laughing anymore. He looked silly wearing my net on his head.

I felt a small rumble in my tummy.

It began to bubble up inside me. Then
I burst out laughing. I hadn't laughed
that hard in a long time.

Dad didn't laugh. He just struggled to get the net off.

"I found my funny bone," I laughed.
Either that or I found my dad's.

GLOSSARY

circus
a big fair

funny bone
a sense of humor

rumble
a low, rolling sound

searched
looked carefully for something

snort
make a laughing noise

struggled
made a big effort

set
to get a trap ready

Christopher Stitt

Christopher has been writing children's stories for many years. He enjoys reading children's books, as well as writing them. He loves to travel, and Africa is his favorite destination. Christopher also enjoys going to the movies and listening to loud music— the louder the better. He's acted in some stage productions. He's written for theater, too.

Nathan Jurevicius

Since the age of six, Nathan has been illustrating funny characters. He loves to draw aliens, bugs, and especially people. Nathan also enjoys traveling with his wife, Liz, and young son, Milo.

Published by Sundance Publishing
P.O. Box 1326, 234 Taylor Street, Littleton, MA 01460
800-343-8204

Copyright © text Christopher Stitt
Copyright © illustrations Nathan Jurevicius

First published 1999 as Sparklers by
Blake Education, Locked Bag 2022, Glebe 2037, Australia
Exclusive United States Distribution: Sundance Publishing

ISBN 0-7608-8000-X

Printed in Canada